To Jamie

For being good.

MERRY CHRISTMAS!

From Santa and
Patrick & Anna - your Aussie
neighbours ♡

Santa is coming to the Outback

LAKE PRESS

Lake Press Pty Ltd
16 Sandilands Street
South Melbourne VIC 3205 Australia
Email: publishing@lakepress.com.au
www.lakepress.com.au

Written by Steve Smallman
Illustrated by Robert Dunn
Designed by Sarah Allen

First published 2013
Printed in China 5 4 3 2 1
LP14 034

Santa is coming to the Outback

Written by Steve Smallman

Illustrated by Robert Dunn

ALiCAT

"Well?"

boomed Santa. "Have all the children from **the outback** been good this year?"

"Well...uh...mostly," answered the little old elf, as he bustled across the busy workshop to Santa's desk.

Santa peered down at the elf from behind the tall, teetering piles of letters that the children from the outback had sent him.

"Mostly?" asked Santa, looking over the top of his glasses.

"Yes...but they've all been **especially** good in the last few days!" said the elf.

"Jolly good!" chuckled Santa.
"Then we'd better get their presents loaded up!"

Even though the sack of presents was

really, really big

and the elves were really, really small,

they seemed to have no trouble loading it onto Santa's sleigh.
Though how they managed to fit such a big sack into one little sleigh
even they didn't know. But somehow they did.

"Splendid!" boomed Santa. "We're ready to go!"

"Er...not quite, Santa," said the little old elf. "One of our reindeer is missing!"

"Missing?

Which reindeer is missing?" asked Santa.

"The youngest one, Santa," said the elf. "It's his first flight tonight. I've called him and called him, but..."

Just then, a young reindeer strolled up, munching on a large carrot.

"Where have you been?"

asked Santa.

But the youngest reindeer was crunching so loudly that it was no wonder he hadn't heard the little old elf calling.

"Oh well, never mind," said Santa, giving the reindeer a little wink.
He took out his Santa-nav and tapped in the coordinates for the outback.
"This will guide us to the outback in no time."

Crunch!
Crunch!
Crunch!

With a flick of the reins and a jerk of the harness, off they went, racing through the sky.

"Ho, ho, ho!"

laughed Santa.

"We'll soon have these presents delivered all over the outback!"

Santa's sleigh flew through the starry night heading south. On they flew as the crisp, wintry night turned to daylight. In the wink of an eye, the sleigh crossed over the Equator and headed down to Australia.

The youngest reindeer was very excited. He had never been away from the North Pole before.

They had just crossed the Darwin coastline
when, suddenly, they ran into thick cloud.

They couldn't see a thing!

The youngest reindeer was getting a bit worried,
but Santa didn't seem worried at all.

"In two kilometres..."

said the Santa-nav in a bossy lady's voice,

"...keep left at the next star."

"But, madam," Santa blustered, "I can't see any stars in all this cloud!"
Soon they were

hopelessly lost!

Om-ohm!
Om-ohm!

Then, through the heavy cloud, the youngest reindeer heard a deep droning sound.

Om-ohm!

He looked over at the old reindeer with the red nose. But he had his head down.

(Red nose...I wonder who that could be?!)

Om-ohm!
Om-ohm!

Om-ohm!
Om-ohm!

There was that sound again, like a deep fog horn. The youngest reindeer turned around to look at Santa, but Santa wasn't listening. He seemed to be arguing with a little box with buttons on it.

With a flick of the harness and a jerk of the reins, the youngest reindeer gave a sharp *tug* and headed off towards the sound of the droning noise, pulling Santa and his sleigh behind him!

"Whoa!

cried Santa, pulling his hat straight.
"What's going on?" Then, to his surprise,
he heard the droning sound.

"Well done, young reindeer!" he shouted
cheerfully, "It must be someone playing a didgeridoo.
Don't worry, children, Santa is coming!"

Then, suddenly...

CRUNCH!

The sleigh hit something as it plummeted through the cloud. **"You have arrived!"** said the Santa-nav unhelpfully.

Finally, when the clouds parted, Santa
discovered where "arrived" was...

...stuck, right on the very
top of Uluru!

"Everybody,
PULL!"

The reindeer *pulled* with all their might until, at last, with a screeching noise, the sleigh scraped clear of the great rock. Santa steered them safely over the Olgas, past Kings Canyon and over Alice Springs until he could stop safely in front of an old shearing shed.

Luckily, there was no
real damage done, but the
packages had all been jumbled
up. Santa quickly sorted the
presents into order again.

"All right," said Santa. "Thanks to this
young reindeer I know where we are now.
Don't worry, children,

Santa is coming!"

Santa drove his sleigh expertly from rooftop to rooftop all over the outback, popping in and out of chimneys as fast as he could go.

(Which was pretty fast for a chubby fellow!)

Sometimes there were many hundreds of kilometres between houses, but Santa worked at the speed of lightning, placing presents under every Christmas tree in the outback.

The youngest reindeer was amazed at how quickly they went. Santa never seemed to get tired at all! And it looked like the children in the outback were going to be very lucky this year! But the youngest reindeer was starting to feel a bit weary and quite hungry too!

He piled them under the Christmas trees and carefully filled up the stockings with surprises.

In house after house, Santa delved inside his sack for packages of every shape and size.

Santa took a little bite out of each cookie, a tiny sip of milk, wiped his beard, and popped the carrots into his sack.

In house after house, the good children of the Aussie outback had left out a plate of cookies, a small glass of milk and a big, crunchy carrot.

From Katherine to Oodnadatta, from Port Hedland to Longreach, and all the places in between, Santa and his sleigh visited every house in the outback.

Finally, Santa had delivered the last present on his long Aussie outback list.

"Great moons and stars!" sighed Santa. "It's nearly morning and my sack seems as heavy as ever! I hope I haven't forgotten anyone."

Santa opened his sack to check...but it was full of juicy, crunchy carrots!

Santa divided the carrots among all the reindeer.
"Well done!" he said, patting the youngest reindeer
gently on the nose.

But the youngest reindeer didn't hear him...he was too busy munching!

It was time to set off for home. Santa reset his Santa-nav once more to the North Pole,
and soon they were speeding past the Simpson Desert, over the MacDonnell Ranges,
high above the Kimberleys and into the rapidly approaching dawn.